Hiccups

Written by Amy H. Sacco
Illustrated by
Jessie Nixon

Hiccups

This book is published and distributed by Lakshmi Books.
For information or to order bulk copies of this book, please contact the publisher at:
Lakshmi Books
P.O. Box 1205
Leominster, MA 01453

Illustrated by Jessie Nixon
May 2013

ISBN: 978-1-62728-007-5
Library of Congress Control Number: 2013939849

In memory of my grandmothers,
who taught me just how much
fun words can be.

Robbie had the hiccups at

least five times a day.

"We don't know what

causes them," he

heard the doctors say.

He would hiccup all day long and hiccup through the night. His relatives had the cures that they thought were just right!

"Drink your juice upside down," his Mommy would say. Juice came out his nose. They did not go away.

"I'll jump out and scare you,"

his Daddy would

say. But it just made him

frightened. They did not

go away.

"A nice teaspoon of sugar,"

his Grandma would say.

But he made a silly face.

They did not go away.

“Bounce up and down,”his uncle would say. But it just made him tired. They did not go away.

Robbie tried each cure, one at a time. Then his Grandpa yelled from the tub, "well, he hasn't tried mine!"

Now his Grandpa was a

silly man who had ideas

so grand:

Just by holding drums and

horns, he thought he could

make a band.

By thinking, wishing, simply

placing stamps upon his knees,

he thought that he could

mail himself anywhere he

pleased.

So with a towel around his middle and suds upon his head, he leapt out of the tub and this is what he said:

"The sugar was much too sweet, the juice came out his nose. The scaring was just too frightening and the bouncing hurt his toes!"

So his Grandpa had a

crazy thought, "do them all

at once!"

Then the relatives said

together "yes, do them

in a bunch!"

"He'll be scared and he will bounce, and on juice and sugar he will dine. He should try all these cures, all at the very same time!"

Robbie listened carefully and did as Grandpa said, because nothing else worked thus far, and it was time to go to bed.

So he grabbed a scoop of sugar and gulped a glass of juice.

His daddy gave him such

a scare, he jumped over

his toy caboose.

And then it all went quiet, as
the group waited to see
if the hiccups had been
cured, if silent he would
be. Not a single sound was
heard. The hiccups went away.

And Robbie fell fast asleep. He'd had a busy day.

"A-choo...uh oh!"